WILD RIVER ADVENTURE

Based on the TV series *Nickelodeon Rocket Power*™ created by Klasky Csupo, Inc.
as seen on Nickelodeon®

SIMON SPOTLIGHT
An imprint of Simon & Schuster Children's Publishing Division
1230 Avenue of the Americas, New York, New York 10020

Manufactured in the United States of America

2 4 6 8 10 9 7 5 3

Library of Congress Cataloging-in-Publication Data
Banks, Steven.
Wild river adventure / by Steven Banks.—1st ed.
p. cm. — (Rocket Power ready-to-read ; #2)
"Based on the TV series Nickelodeon Rocket PowerTM created by
Klasky Csupo, Inc. as seen on Nickelodeon."
Summary: Otto and Reggie are excited about racing their kayak down the Wild
River, but they get distracted when their friend Sam thinks he sees Big Toe in the
nearby woods.
ISBN 0-689-85009-3
[1. Kayaking—Fiction. 2. Fear—Fiction.] I. Title. II. Series.
PZ7.B22637 Wi 2002
[E]—dc21
2002001136

WILD RIVER ADVENTURE

by
Steven Banks

illustrated by
Pilar Newton-Mitchell

Simon Spotlight/Nickelodeon

New York   London   Toronto   Sydney   Singapore

"Wild River, here we come!" Reggie cried.
Reggie and Otto were going on a river trip
in the mountains with their dad, Ray.
Their friends Twister and Sam
were coming along too.
"We are going to set the record for the
fastest trip down the river!" said Otto.

"And I am going to get
the best video ever," said Twister.
"Maybe I will even get
a shot of Big Toe!"

"Big Toe? What's Big Toe?" asked Sam.
"Everybody around here knows
 about Big Toe," said Twister. "He's a big,
 scary monster dude that lives in the woods."
"Big Toe isn't for real," Reggie said.
"Oh, yes, he is," Twister argued, "and I will
 prove it by getting a shot of him!"

Ray parked the car near Wild River.
"I do not think I want to meet Big Toe," said Sam.
"You will not, because there's no such thing!"
Reggie said.
"Who cares?" Otto asked. "We have
a wild river to tame!"

"Hey, kids, my old friend Derek lives up here,"
said Ray. "I will go see him while you guys
go down the river. Remember, stay safe.
I will meet you back here in an hour."
"Catch you later," called Reggie.
"Unless Big Toe gets to us first," Otto said,
chuckling.

Otto and Reggie went down the river
while Twister filmed from the riverbank.
Sam kept an eye out for anything strange.

"Watch out!" Reggie exclaimed.
"No problem!" said Otto,
 as they sailed smoothly over the waterfall.
"Woo-hoo!"

Meanwhile Sam was so busy looking for
Big Toe that he bumped into Twister.
Twister fell and almost dropped his camera.
"Whoa!" he cried.
"Sorry, Twister. I thought I saw something,"
said Sam.
"Was it Big Toe?" asked Twister.
"I hope not!" said Sam.

The river went through a dark cave.
"Keep paddling!" yelled Otto,
 as a bat flew over their heads.
"Even though there's no such thing
 as Big Toe, I still wouldn't want
 to meet him in here," Reggie said.

Otto and Reggie quickly reached
the end of the river.
Reggie looked at her watch. "That took
fifteen minutes and ten seconds."
"Aww . . . we can beat that," said Otto.
"Let's go again!"

"Hey, Twist, did you get us going
over the waterfall?" asked Otto
when they met up with their friends.
"No," said Twister. "I kind of fell down.
Sam bumped into me.
He thought he saw Big Toe."

"Let's look at what I taped," said Twister.

"Well, you got us racing down the river," Reggie said.

"Hey, what's that in the trees?" asked Sam. They took a closer look. Way in the corner of the screen was a huge, strange-looking figure.

"It's Big Toe!" shouted Twister. "I got him on tape! I proved it—Big Toe is real!"

"Reggie, you said there was no such thing!" said Sam.

"There isn't . . . I think," Reggie said.

"I want to find Big Toe!" said Twister.

"I want to go down the river again!" said Otto.

"I want to go home!" cried Sam.

Sam started to walk back to the car.
"Wait, Sam! Come back!" called Reggie.
"No way! I am getting out of here!"
said Sam. But then he stopped.
There in the dirt was the biggest footprint
he had ever seen!
"Uh . . . guys," Sam said, "come look at this . . ."

"It's Big Toe's footprint!" Twister yelled.
Reggie looked closer at the footprint.
"Hmm . . . Big Toe seems to be wearing sneakers."
"That means he can run fast. Let's motor!"
Sam cried.

Suddenly they heard a rustling noise in the trees.
Something was coming toward them!

"Hey, kids! How are you doing?"
called a big booming voice.
It was a man who looked to be
almost eight feet tall!

"My name's Derek Hightower," said the man.
"I have heard of you," said Otto.
"You used to play basketball."
"I sure did. For twelve years. Then I retired here
to the mountains," Derek said.
Just then there was another rustling in the trees.

But it was only Ray.

"Well, I see you guys have met my friend
Derek 'Big Man' Hightower," he said.
"The greatest center in basketball!"

"We met him all right," said Sam,
"and we are glad he's not Big Toe!"

Derek laughed. "Well, I do have big toes!"

"How about a race down the river?"
asked Derek.
"Your dad says you are pretty fast!"
"You got it!" Otto said.
Ray and Derek got into one kayak.
Otto and Reggie got into the other.

"On your mark, get set, GO!"
shouted Sam.

Derek and Ray paddled hard—too hard!
They soon tipped over and got all wet.
But Otto and Reggie kept paddling
and won the race!
"Rocket power!" shouted Otto.